James Parton

Revolutionary Heroes

And Other Historical Papers

James Parton

Revolutionary Heroes
And Other Historical Papers

ISBN/EAN: 9783337195601

Printed in Europe, USA, Canada, Australia, Japan

Cover: Foto ©Andreas Hilbeck / pixelio.de

More available books at **www.hansebooks.com**

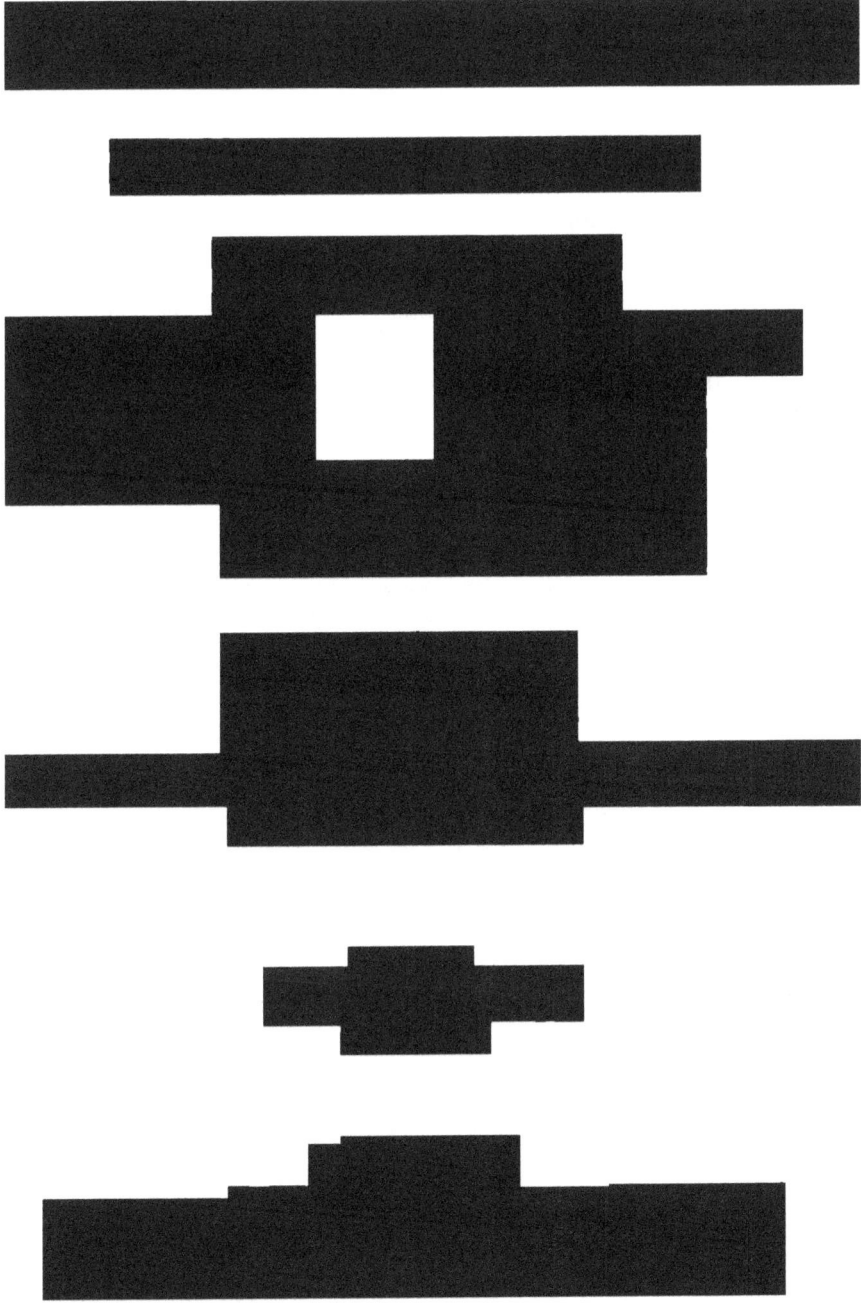

INTRODUCTION.

JAMES PARTON was born in Canterbury, England, February 9, 1822. When five years old he was brought to America and given an education in the schools of New York City, and at White Plains, N. Y. Subsequently he engaged in teaching in Philadelphia and New York City, and for three years was a contributor to the *Home Journal.* Since that time, he has devoted his life to literary labors, contributing many articles to periodicals and publishing books on biographical subjects. While employed on the *Home Journal* it occurred to him that an interesting story could be made out of the life of Horace Greeley, and he mentioned the idea to a New York publisher. Receiving the needed encouragement, Mr. Parton set about collecting material from Greeley's former neighbors in Vermont and New Hampshire, and in 1855 produced the " Life of Horace Greeley," which he afterwards extended and completed in 1885. This venture was so profitable that he was encouraged to devote himself to authorship. In 1856 he brought out a collection of Humorous Poetry of the English Language from Chaucer to Saxe. Following this appeared in 1857 the " Life of Aaron Burr," prepared from original sources and intended to redeem Burr's reputation from the charges that attached to his memory. In writing the " Life of Andrew Jackson " he also had access to original and unpublished documents. This work was published in three volumes in 1859–60. Other works of later publication are: " General Butler in New Orleans " (1863 and 1882); " Life and Times of Benjamin Franklin " (1864); " How New York is Governed " (1866); "Famous Americans of

3

Recent Times," containing Sketches of Henry Clay, Daniel Webster, John C. Calhoun, John Randolph, and others (1867); "The People's Book of Biography," containing eighty short lives (1868); "Smoking and Drinking," an essay on the evils of those practices, reprinted from the *Atlantic Monthly* (1869); a pamphlet entitled "The Danish Islands: Are We Bound to Pay for Them?" (1869); "Topics of the Time," a collection of magazine articles, most of them treating of administrative abuses at Washington (1871); "Triumphs of Enterprise, Ingenuity, and Public Spirit" (1871); "The Words of Washington" (1872); "Fanny Fern," a memorial volume (1873); "Life of Thomas Jefferson, Third President of the United States" (1874); "Taxation of Church Property" (1874); "La Parnasse Français: a Book of French Poetry from A.D. 1850 to the Present Time" (1877); "Caricature and other Comic Art in All Times and Many Lands" (1877); "A Life of Voltaire," which was the fruit of several years' labor (1881); "Noted Women of Europe and America" (1883); and "Captains of Industry, or Men of Business who did something besides Making Money: a Book for Young Americans." In addition to his writing Mr. Parton has proved a very successful lecturer on literary and political topics.

In January, 1856, Mr. Parton married Sara Payson Willis, a sister of the poet N. P. Willis, and herself famous as "Fanny Fern," the name of her pen. He made New York City his home until 1875, three years after the death of his wife, when he went to Newburyport, where he now lives. *The London Athenæum* well characterizes Mr. Parton as "a painstaking, honest, and courageous historian, ardent with patriotism, but unprejudiced; a writer, in short, of whom the people of the United States have reason to be proud."

The contents of this book have been selected from among the great number contributed from time to time by Mr. Parton, and are considered as particularly valuable and interesting reading.

REVOLUTIONARY HEROES.

GENERAL JOSEPH WARREN.

A FIERY, vehement, daring spirit was this Joseph Warren, who was a doctor thirteen years, a major-general three days, and a soldier three hours.

In that part of Boston which is called Roxbury, there is a modern house of stone, on the front of which a passer-by may read the following inscription:

"On this spot stood the house erected in 1720 by Joseph Warren, of Boston, remarkable for being the birth-place of General Joseph Warren, his grandson, who was killed at the battle of Bunker Hill, June 17, 1775."

There is another inscription on the house which reads thus:

"John Warren, a distinguished Physician and Anatomist, was also born here. The original mansion being in ruins, this house was built by John C. Warren, M.D., in 1846, son of the last-named, as a permanent memorial of the spot."

I am afraid the builder of this new house *poetized* a little when he styled the original edifice a mansion. It was a plain, roomy, substantial farm-house, about the centre of the little village of Roxbury, and the father of Warren who occupied it was an industrious, enterprising, intelligent farmer, who raised superior fruits and vegetables for the Boston market. Warren's father was a beginner in that delightful industry, and one of the apples which he introduced into the neighborhood retains to this day the name which it bore in his lifetime, the Warren Russet.

A tragic event occurred at this farm-house in 1775, when Warren was a boy of fourteen. It was on an October day, in the midst of the apple-gathering season, about the time when the Warren Russet had attained all the maturity it can upon its native tree. Farmer Warren was out in his orchard. His wife, a woman worthy of being the mother of such a son as she had, was indoors getting dinner ready for her husband, her four boys, and the two laborers upon the farm. About noon she sent her youngest son, John, mentioned in the above inscription, to call his father to dinner. On the way to the orchard the lad met the two laborers carrying towards the house his father's dead body. While standing upon a ladder gathering apples from a high tree, Mr. Warren had fallen to the ground and broken his neck. He died almost instantly.

The *Boston Newsletter* of the following week bestowed a few lines upon the occurrence ; speaking of him as a man of good understanding, industrious, honest and faithful ; "a useful member of society, who was generally respected among us, and whose death is universally lamented."

Fortunate is the family which in such circumstances has a mother wise and strong. She carried on the farm with the assistance of one of her sons so successfully that she was able to continue the education of her children, all of whom except the farmer obtained respectable rank in one of the liberal professions. This excellent mother lived in widowhood nearly fifty years, saw Thomas Jefferson President of the United States, and died 1803, aged ninety-three years, in the old house at home. Until she was past eighty she made with her own hands the pies for Thanksgiving-day, when all her children and grandchildren used to assemble at the spacious old Roxbury house.

It was in the very year of his father's death, 1755, that Joseph Warren entered Harvard College, a vigorous, handsome lad of fourteen, noted even then for his spirit, courage and resolution. Several of his class one day, in the course of a frolic, in order to exclude him from the fun, barred the door so that he could not force it. Determined to join them, he went to the roof of the house, slid down by the spout, and sprang through the open window into the room. At that moment the spout fell to the ground.

" It has served my purpose," said the youth coolly.

The records of the college show that he held respectable rank as a student; and as soon as he had graduated, he received an appointment which proves that he was held in high estimation in his native village. We find him at nineteen master of the Roxbury Grammar School, at a salary of forty-four pounds and sixteen shillings per annum, payable to his mother. A receipt for part of this amount, signed by his mother and in her handwriting, is now among the archives of that ancient and famous institution. He taught one year, at the end of which he entered the office of a Boston physician, under whom he pursued the usual medical studies and was admitted to practice.

The young doctor, tall, handsome, alert, graceful, full of energy and fire, was formed to succeed in such a community as that of Boston. His friends, when he was twenty-three years of age, had the pleasure of reading in the Boston newspaper the following notice :

" Last Thursday evening was married Dr. Joseph Warren, one of the physicians of this town, to Miss Elizabeth Hooton, only daughter of the late Mr. Richard Hooton, merchant, deceased, an accomplished young lady with a handsome fortune."

Thus launched in life and gifted as he was, it is not surprising that he should soon have attained a considerable practice. But for one circumstance he would have advanced in his profession even more rapidly than he did. When he had been but a few months married, the Stamp Act was passed, which began the long series of agitating events that ended in severing the colonies from the mother country. The wealthy society of Boston, from the earliest period down to the present hour, has always been on what is called the conservative side in politics; and it was eminently so during the troubles preceding the revolutionary war. The whole story is told in a remark made by a Boston Tory doctor in those times:

"If Warren were not a Whig," said he, "he might soon be independent and ride in his chariot."

There were, however, in Boston Whig families enough to give him plenty of business, and he was for many years their favorite physician. He attended the family of John Adams, and saved John Quincy, his son, from losing one of his fore-fingers when it was very badly fractured. Samuel Adams, who was the prime mover of the Opposition, old enough to be his father, inspired and consulted him. Gradually, as the quarrel grew warmer, Dr. Warren was drawn into the councils of the leading Whigs, and became at last almost wholly a public man. Without being rash or imprudent, he was one of the first to be ready to meet force with force, and he was always in favor of the measures which were boldest and most decisive. At his house Colonel Putnam was a guest on an interesting occasion, when he was only known for his exploits in the French war.

"The old hero, Putnam," says a Boston letter of 1774, "arrived in town on Monday, bringing with him one hundred and thirty sheep from the little parish of Brooklyn."

It was at Dr. Warren's house that the "old hero" staid, and thither flocked crowds of people to see him, and talk over the thrilling events of the time. The sheep which he brought with him were to feed the people of Boston, whose business was suspended by the closing of the port.

The presence of the British troops in Boston roused all Warren's indignation. Overhearing one day some British officers saying that the Americans would not fight, he said to a friend;

"These fellows say we will not fight. By heavens, I hope I shall die up to my knees in their blood!"

Soon after, as he was passing the public gallows on the Neck, he overheard one of a group of officers say in an insulting tone:

"Go on, Warren; you will soon come to the gallows."

The young doctor turned, walked up to the officers, and said to them quietly:

"Which of you uttered those words."

They passed on without giving any reply. He had not long to wait for a proof that his countrymen would fight. April nineteenth, 1775, word was brought to him by a special messenger of the events which had occurred on the village green at Lexington. He called to his assistant, told him to take care of his patients, mounted his horse, and rode toward the scene of action.

"Keep up a brave heart!" he cried to a friend in passing. "They have begun it. *That* either party can do. And we will end it. *That* only one can do."

Riding fast, he was soon in the thick of the melée, and kept so close to the point of contact that a British musket ball struck a pin out of his hair close to one of his ears. Wherever the danger was greatest there was Warren, now a soldier joining in the fight, now a surgeon binding up wounds, now a citizen cheering on his fellows. From this day he made up his mind to perform his part in the coming contest as a soldier, not as a physician, nor in any civil capacity; and accordingly on the fourteenth of June, 1775, the Massachu-

setts legislature elected him " second Major-General of the
Massachusetts army." Before he had received his commission occurred the battle of Bunker Hill, June seventeenth.
He passed the night previous in public service, for he was
President of the Provincial Congress, but, on the seventeenth,
when the congress met at Watertown, the president did not
appear. Members knew where he was, for he had told his
friends that he meant to take part in the impending movement.

It was a burning hot summer's day. After his night of
labor, Warren threw himself on his bed, sick from a nervous
headache. The booming of the guns summoned him forth,
and shortly before the first assault he was on the field ready
to serve.

" I am here," he said to General Putnam, " only as a volunteer. Tell me where I can be most useful."

And to Colonel Prescott he said :

"I shall take no command here. I come as a volunteer,
with my musket to serve under you."

And there he fought during the three onsets, cheering
the men by his coolness and confidence. He was one of the
the very last to leave the redoubt. When he had retreated
about sixty yards he was recognized by a British officer, who
snatched a musket from a soldier and shot him. The bullet
entered the back of his head. Warren placed his hands, as
if mechanically, to the wound, and fell dead upon the hot
and dusty field.

The enemy buried him where he fell. Nine months after,
when the British finally retreated from New England, his
body, recognized by two false teeth, was disinterred and
honorably buried. He left four children, of whom the
eldest was a girl six years of age. Congress adopted the
eldest son. Among those who contributed most liberally
toward the education and support of the other children was

Benedict Arnold, who gave five hundred dollars. A little psalm book found by a British soldier in Warren's pocket on the field is still in possession of one of his descendants.

Captain Nathan Hale, the Martyr-Spy.

General Washington wanted a man. It was in September, 1776, at the City of New York, a few days after the battle of Long Island. The swift and deep East River flowed between the two hostile armies, and General Washington had as yet no system established for getting information of the enemy's movements and intentions. He never needed such information so much as at that crisis.

What would General Howe do next? If he crossed at Hell Gate, the American army, too small in numbers, and defeated the week before, might be caught on Manhattan Island as in a trap, and the issue of the contest might be made to depend upon a single battle; for in such circumstances defeat would involve the capture of the whole army. And yet General Washington was compelled to confess:

" We cannot learn, nor have we been able to procure the least information of late."

Therefore he wanted a man. He wanted an intelligent man, cool-headed, skillful, brave, to cross the East River to Long Island, enter the enemy's camp, and get information as to his strength and intentions. He went to Colonel Knowlton, commanding a remarkably efficient regiment from Connecticut, and requested him to ascertain if this man, so sorely needed, could be found in his command. Colonel Knowlton called his officers together, stated the wishes of General Washington, and, without urging the enterprise upon any individual, left the matter to their reflections.

Captain Nathan Hale, a brilliant youth of twenty-one, recently graduated from Yale College, was one of those who reflected upon the subject. He soon reached a conclusion. He was of the very flower of the young men of New England, and one of the best of the younger soldiers of the patriot army. He had been educated for the ministry, and his motive in adopting for a time the profession of arms was purely patriotic. This we know from the familiar records of his life at the time when the call to arms was first heard.

In addition to his other gifts and graces, he was handsome, vigorous, and athletic, all in an extraordinary degree. If he had lived in our day he might have pulled the stroke-oar at New London, or pitched for the college nine.

The officers were conversing in a group. No one had as yet spoken the decisive word. Colonel Knowlton appealed to a French sergeant, an old soldier of former wars, and asked him to volunteer.

" No, no," said he. " I am ready to fight the British at any place and time, but I do not feel willing to go among them to be hung up like a dog."

Captain Hale joined the group of officers. He said to Colonel Knowlton :

" I will undertake it."

Some of his best friends remonstrated. One of them, afterwards the famous general William Hull, then a captain in Washington's army, has recorded Hale's reply to his own attempt to dissuade him.

" I think," said Hale, " I owe to my country the accomplishment of an object so important. I am fully sensible of the consequences of discovery and capture in such a situation. But for a year I have been attached to the army, and have not rendered any material service, while receiving a compensation for which I make no return. I wish to be useful, and every kind of service necessary for the public good becomes honorable by being necessary."

He spoke, as General Hull remembered, with earnestness and decision, as one who had considered the matter well, and had made up his mind.

Having received his instructions, he traveled fifty miles along the Sound as far as Norwalk in Connecticut. One who saw him there made a very wise remark upon him, to the effect that he was "too good-looking" to go as a spy. He could not deceive. "Some scrubby fellow ought to have gone." At Norwalk he assumed the disguise of a Dutch schoolmaster, putting on a suit of plain brown clothes, and a round, broad-brimmed hat. He had no difficulty in crossing the Sound, since he bore an order from General Washington which placed at his disposal all the vessels belonging to Congress. For several days everything appears to have gone well with him, and there is reason to believe that he passed through the entire British army without detection or even exciting suspicion.

Finding the British had crossed to New York, he followed them. He made his way back to Long Island, and nearly reached the point opposite Norwalk where he had originally landed. Rendered perhaps too bold by success, he went into a well-known and popular tavern, entered into conversation with the guests, and made himself very agreeable. The tradition is that he made himself too agreeable. A man present suspecting or knowing that he was not the character he had assumed, quietly left the room, communicated his suspicions to the captain of a British ship anchored near, who dispatched a boat's crew to capture and bring on board the agreeable stranger. His true character was immediately revealed. Drawings of some of the British works, with notes in Latin, were found hidden in the soles of his shoes. Nor did he attempt to deceive his captors, and the English captain, lamenting, as he said, that "so fine a fellow had fallen into his power," sent him to New York in one of his boats, and with him the fatal proofs that he was a spy.

September twenty-first was the day on which he reached New York—the day of the great fire which laid one-third of the little city in ashes. From the time of his departure from General Washington's camp to that of his return to New York was about fourteen days. He was taken to General Howe's headquarters at the Beekman mansion, on the East River, near the corner of the present Fifty-first Street and First Avenue. It is a strange coincidence that this house to which he was brought to be tried as a spy was the very one from which Major André departed when he went to West Point. Tradition says that Captain Hale was examined in a greenhouse which then stood in the garden of the Beekman mansion.

Short was his trial, for he avowed at once his true character. The British general signed an order to his provost-marshal directing him to receive into his custody the prisoner convicted as a spy, and to see him hanged by the neck "to-morrow morning at daybreak."

Terrible things are reported of the manner in which this noble prisoner, this admirable gentleman and hero, was treated by his jailer and executioner. There are savages in every large army, and it is possible that this provost-marshal was one of them. It is said that he refused him writing-materials, and afterwards, when Captain Hale had been furnished them by others. destroyed before his face his last letters to his mother and to the young lady to whom he was engaged to be married. As those letters were never received this statement may be true. The other alleged horrors of the execution it is safe to disregard, because we know that it was conducted in the usual form and in the presence of many spectators and a considerable body of troops. One fact shines out from the distracting confusion of that morning, which will be cherished to the latest posterity as a precious ingot of the moral treasure of the American people. When asked if he had anything to say, Captain Hale replied :

" I only regret that I have but one life to lose for my country."

The scene of his execution was probably an old graveyard in Chambers Street, which was then called Barrack Street. General Howe formally notified General Washington of his execution. In recent years, through the industry of investigators, the pathos and sublimity of these events have been in part revealed.

In 1887 a bronze statue of the young hero was unveiled in the State House at Hartford. Mr. Charles Dudley Warner delivered a beautiful address suitable to the occasion, and Governor Lounsberry worthily accepted the statue on behalf of the State. It is greatly to be regretted that our knowledge of this noble martyr is so slight ; but we know enough to be sure that he merits the veneration of his countrymen.

General Washington's Other Spies.

THE reader would scarcely expect at this late day to get new light upon the military character of General Washington. But, in truth, scarcely a month passes in which some of our busy historical students do not add to our knowledge of him. Recently Mr. H. P. Johnston published in the *Magazine of American History* some curious documents, hitherto unknown, exhibiting Washington's methods of procuring intelligence of the movements of the British army.

Like a true general, he knew from the first all the importance of correct and prompt information. How necessary this is, is known to every one who remembers vividly the late war, particularly the first few months of it, before there was any good system of employing spies. Some terrible disasters could have been avoided if our generals had obtained better information of the opposing army's position, temper, and resources.

An attentive study of the dispatches of Napoleon Bonaparte will show the importance which he attached to intelligence of this kind. He kept near him at headquarters an officer of rank who had nothing to do but to procure, record, and arrange all the military news which could be gleaned from newspapers, correspondents, and spies. The name of every regiment, detachment, and corps in the enemy's service was written upon a card. For the reception of these cards he had a case made with compartments and pigeon-holes. Every time a movement was reported the cards were shifted to correspond, so that he could know at a glance, when the cards were spread out upon a table, just how the troops of the enemy were distributed or massed. Every few days, the officer in charge had to send the emperor a list of the changes which had taken place. This important matter was intrusted to a person who knew the languages of the different nations engaged in the war.

It was Bonaparte's perfect organization of his spy system which enabled him to carry out his plan of always having a superior force at the point of attack. These two were the great secrets of his tactical system, namely, to have the best information and the most men at the decisive moment.

Bonaparte was a trained soldier; but when Washington took command of the army in July, 1775, he had had very little experience of actual warfare. That little, however, was precisely of the kind to prove the value of correct information. For the want of it, he had seen General Braddock lead an army into the jaws of destruction, and he may have still possessed in some closet of Mount Vernon the coat with four bullet-holes in it which he had himself worn on that occasion. There are no warriors so skillful either at getting or concealing information as Indians, and all his experience hitherto had been in the Indian country and with warlike methods of an Indian character.

Hence it is not surprising to discover that the first important act which he performed at Cambridge was to engage a person to go into the city of Boston for the purpose of procuring "intelligence of the enemy's movements and designs." An entry in his private note-book shows that he paid this unknown individual $333.33 in advance.

A person who serves as a spy takes his life in his hand. It is a curious fact of human nature that nothing so surely reconciles a man to risking his life as a handsome sum in cash. General Washington, being perfectly aware of this fact, generally contrived to have a sum of what he called "hard money" at headquarters all through the war. Spies do not readily take to paper money. There are no Greenbackers among them. In the letters of General Washington we find a great many requests to Congress for a kind of money that would pass current anywhere, and suffer no deterioration at the bottom of a river in a freshet. He preferred gold as being the "most portable." He wrote in 1778 from White Plains:

"I have always found a difficulty in procuring intelligence by the means of paper money, and I perceive that it increases."

It continued to increase, until, I suppose, an offer of a million dollars in paper would not have induced a spy to enter the enemy's lines. In fact, the general himself says as much. In acknowledging the receipt of five hundred guineas for the secret service, he says that for want of a little gold he had been obliged to dispense with the services of some of his informers; and adds:

" In some cases no consideration in paper money has been found sufficient to effect even an engagement to procure intelligence; and where it has been otherwise, the terms of service on account of the depreciation have been high, if not exorbitant."

The time was not distant when paper money ceased to have any value, and Governor Jefferson of Virginia paid his whole salary for a year (a thousand pounds) for a second-hand side-saddle.

During the later years of the war, the city of New York was the chief source of information concerning the designs and movements of the enemy. General Washington, as early as 1778, had always two or three correspondents there upon whose information he could rely if only they could send it out to him. Sometimes, when his ordinary correspondents failed him, he would send in a spy disguised as a farmer driving a small load of provisions, and who would bring out some family supplies, as tea, sugar, and calico, the better to conceal his real object. Often the spy *was* a farmer, and sometimes quite illiterate. As it was unsafe for him to have any written paper upon his person, he was required to learn by heart the precise message which he was to deliver in the city, as also the information which he received from the resident correspondent.

The messenger frequently entered the city in the disguise of a peddler, a fact which suggested to Horace Greeley, when he was a printer's apprentice in Vermont, the idea of a story which he called " The Peddler-Spy of the Revolution." I once had in my hand a considerable package of his manuscript of this tale; but even as a boy he wrote so bad a hand that I could not read much of it. It is possible that this manuscript still exists.

These methods of procuring intelligence in New York were all abused by real peddlers, who, when they were caught selling contraband goods to the enemy, pretended to be spies, and so escaped the penalty. At length the general chiefly depended upon two persons, one called "Culper Senior," and the other "Culper Junior," who may have been father and son, but whose real names and qualities have never been disclosed. General Washington's secrecy was perfect. His most confidential officers, except one or two who had to be in the secret, never knew enough of these men to be able to designate them afterwards. When Benedict Arnold fled to New York after his treason, the American spies there were panic-stricken, as they very naturally concluded that Arnold must have been acquainted with their names and residences. General Washington was able to assure them that such was not the fact, and it is even probable that only one individual besides himself knew who they were. This was Major Benjamin Tallmadge, a native of Long Island, who frequently received the dispatches from New York and forwarded them to headquarters. The letters were commonly taken across the East River to Brooklyn; thence to a point on the Sound about opposite to Rye or Portchester; and were thence conveyed to camp.

The dispatches from the Culpers were generally written in invisible ink, which was made legible by wetting the paper with another liquid. It was a matter of no small difficulty to keep the spies in New York supplied with the two fluids, and also with the guineas which were requisite for their maintenance. At first the spies wrote their letters on a blank sheet of paper; but that would never do. General Washington wrote:

" This circumstance alone is sufficient to raise suspicions. A much better way is to write a letter in the Tory style, with some mixture of family matters, and, between the lines and on the remaining part of the sheet, communicate with the stain (the invisible ink) the intended intelligence."

The Culpers served faithfully to the end of the war, and finally had the happiness of sending to the general the glorious news that the British army, the fleet, and the Tories were all evidently preparing to depart from the city, which they had held for seven years. Who were these adroit and faithful Culpers? The secret seems to have died with Washington and Tallmadge.

An Historic Christmas Night.

" Christmas Day, at night, one hour before day, is the time fixed upon for our attempt upon Trenton."

In this confused way, December 23, 1776, General Washington wrote from his camp, near Trenton Falls, to Colonel Reed, who was posted at Bristol, a few miles further down the Delaware, guarding an important ford.

Before crossing over to the safe side of this wide stream, about twelve hundred feet wide at Trenton, he gave an order so important that, if he had forgotten or omitted it, nothing could have saved Philadelphia from being captured by the British.

He directed that all the boats and barges of the whole region, for seventy miles, everything that could float and carry a man, should be taken over to the western bank of the river, and there carefully concealed, or closely watched.

All the boats and canoes in the creeks and tributaries

were also secured, and hidden where they could do an enemy no good. There were many large barges then upon the Delaware, used for transporting hay and other produce, some of which could have carried over half a regiment of foot at every trip.

All of these were hidden or guarded, and as soon as General Washington had got his own little army over, he posted a guard at every ford, and kept trustworthy men going up and down the river, to see that the boats were safe.

If any one desires to see General Washington when he displayed his manhood and military genius at their best, let him study the records of his life for the month of December, 1776. The soldier, the statesman, the citizen, the brave, indomitable man, each in turn appears, and shines in the trying hours of that month.

Only the River Delaware separated the hostile armies, and the enemy waited but for the ice to form, in order to add Philadelphia to the list of his summer conquests.

Congress had adjourned from Philadelphia to Baltimore. New Jersey was ravaged by ruthless bands of soldiers. Disaffection was on every side. The winter, prematurely cold, threatened to make an ice-bridge over the stream in ten days, and within about the same time the terms of most of General Washington's troops would expire, and he might be left without even the semblance of an army. "Dire necessity," as he said, compelled a movement of some kind.

Christmas had come. It was a cold, freezing day. There was already a large amount of ice floating by, and heaped up along the shore, in many places rendering access to the water impossible, and in all places difficult.

About four o'clock in the afternoon, the troops were drawn up in parade before their camp at Trenton Falls. They were about twenty-four hundred in number. Every man carried three days' cooked rations, and an ample supply of heavy ammunition. Few of the soldiers were adequately clothed, and their shoes were in such bad condition that Major Wilkinson, who rode behind them to the landing-place, reports that " the snow on the ground was tinged here and there with blood." The cold was increasing. The ice was forming rapidly. The wind was high, and there were signs of a snow-storm.

Boats were in readiness, and about sunset the troops began to cross. The passage was attended with such difficulties as would have deterred men less resolute. The current of the river was exceedingly swift, the cold intense, and, although it was the night of a full moon, the thick snow-clouds made the night dark.

Colonel Knox, afterward General Knox of the Artillery and Secretary of War, rendered efficient service on this occasion. Soldiers from Yankee Marblehead manned many of the boats, and lent the aid of their practiced skill and wiry muscle. Every man worked with a will, and yet it was three o'clock in the morning before the troops were all over.

It was four o'clock before they were formed in two bodies and began to march, one division close along the river, and the other on a parallel road, some little distance in the country.

It had been snowing nearly all night, and about the time when the troops were set in motion the storm increased, the wind rose, and hail was mingled with the snow. The storm blew in the faces of the men and they had nine miles to go before reaching Trenton, where fourteen hundred of the Hessian troops were posted under Colonel Rahl.

Soon after, it was whispered about among the men that the fuses of the best muskets were wet and could not be discharged. Upon this being reported to General Sullivan, he glanced around at Captain St. Clair and asked : " What is to be done ?"

"You have nothing for it," replied St. Clair, "but to push on and charge."

The gallant Stark of Vermont was in command of the advance guard, and perhaps near him marched the father of Daniel Webster. Colonel Stark told his men to get their muskets in the best order they could as they marched, and an officer was sent to inform General Washington of this mishap.

"Tell your General," said the Commander-in-chief, "to use the bayonet and penetrate into the town; the town must be taken, and I am resolved to take it."

The soldiers overheard this reply, as it was given by the aide to General Sullivan, and quietly fixed bayonets without waiting for an order.

About eight in the morning both parties arrived near the village of Trenton. General Washington, who rode near the front of his column, asked a man who was chopping wood by the roadside:

"Which way is the Hessian Picket?"

"I don't know," replied the Jerseyman, unwilling to commit himself.

"You may speak," said one of the American officers, "for that is General Washington."

The man raised his hands to heaven and exclaimed: "God bless and prosper you, sir! The picket is in that house, and the sentry stands near that tree."

General Washington instantly ordered an advance. As his men marched rapidly toward the village with a cheer, Colonel Stark and his band answered the shout and rushed upon the enemy.

The Hessians made a brief attempt at resistance; first, by a wild and useless fire from windows, and then by an attempt to form in the main street of the village. This was at once frustrated by Captain T. Forest, who commanded the battery of six guns which had caused much trouble and delay in crossing the river.

At the same time Captain William Washington and Lieutenant James Monroe, afterward President, ran forward with a party to where the Hessians were attempting to establish a battery, drove the artillerists from their guns, and captured two of them, just as they were ready to be discharged.

Both these young officers were wounded. Colonel Stark during the brief combat, as Wilkinson reports, "dealt death wherever he found resistance, and broke down all opposition before him."

Colonel Rahl, who commanded the post, was roused from a deep sleep by the noise of Washington's fire. He did all that was possible to form his panic-stricken and disordered troops, but soon fell from his horse mortally wounded. From that moment, the day was lost to the Hessians.

During the combat, General Washington remained near Captain Forest's battery, directing the fire. He had just ordered the whole battery, charged with canister, to be turned upon the retreating enemy, when Captain Forest, pointing to the flagstaff near Rahl's headquarters, cried, "Sir, they have struck!"

"Struck!" exclaimed General Washington.

"Yes," said Forest; "their colors are down."

"So they are!" said the commander.

General Washington galloped toward them, followed by all the artillerymen, who wished to see the ceremony of surrender. He rode up to where Colonel Rahl had fallen. The wounded man, assisted by soldiers on each side of him, got upon his feet, and presented his sword to the victor.

At this moment Wilkinson, who had been sent away with orders, returned to his general, and witnessed the surrender. Washington took him by the hand, and said, his countenance beaming with joy: "Major Wilkinson, this is a glorious day for our country!"

In a moment, however, the unfortunate Rahl, who stood near, pale, covered with blood, and still bleeding, appeared to be asking for the assistance which his wounds required.

He was at once conveyed to the house of a good Quaker family near by, where he was visited by General Washington in the course of the day, who did all in his power to soothe the feelings of the dying soldier.

This action, reckoning from the first gun, lasted but thirty-five minutes. On the American side two officers were wounded, two privates were killed, four were wounded, and one was frozen to death. Four stands of colors were captured, besides twelve drums, six brass field-pieces, and twelve hundred muskets. The prisoners were nine hundred and forty-six in number, of whom seventy-eight were wounded. Seventeen of the Hessians were killed, of whom six were officers.

We can scarcely imagine the joy which this victory gave to the people everywhere, as the news slowly made its way. They were in the depths of discouragement. There had been moments when Washington himself almost gave up Philadelphia for lost, and it was from Philadelphia that he drew his most essential supplies.

The capture of the post at Trenton, a thing trifling in itself, changed the mood and temper of both parties, and proved to be the turning-point of the war. It saved Philadelphia for that season, freed New Jersey from the ravages of an insolent and ruthless foe, checked disaffection in minds base or timid, and gave Congress time to prepare for a renewal of the strife as soon as the spring should open.

It was a priceless Christmas present which the general and his steadfast band of patriots gave their country in 1776, and it was followed, a week later, by a New Year's gift of similar purport—the capture of the British post at Princeton.

JOHN ADAMS AND THE QUESTION OF INDEPENDENCE.

IT was an act of something more than courage to vote for Independence in 1776. It was an act of far-sighted wisdom as well, and it was done with the utmost possible deliberation.

The last great debate upon the subject took place on Monday, the first of July, 1776. Fifty-one members were present that morning, a number that must have pretty well filled the square, not very large, room in Independence Hall, which many of our readers visited during the Centennial year.

No spectators were present beyond the officers of the House. John Hancock was in the chairman's seat. In the room overhead the legislature of Pennsylvania was in session. Out of doors, in the public squares and grounds adjacent, troops were drilling, as they had been every day for months past, and a great force of men was at work fortifying the Delaware below the city.

This day had been set apart for the final and decisive consideration of Independence. The draft of the Declaration, as written by Mr. Jefferson, had been handed in three days before, and lay upon the table—perhaps visibly so, as well as in a parliamentary sense.

The question had been discussed, and discussed again, and again discussed, until it seemed to the more ardent minds a waste of breath to argue it further; but it requires time, much time, as well as great patience, to bring a representative body to the point of deciding irrevocably a matter so momentous, involving their own and their country's destiny.

Ought we to sever the tie which binds us to the mother

country? That was not so very difficult to answer; but there was another question : *Can* we? Britain is mighty, and what are we? Thirteen colonies of farmers, with little money, no allies, no saltpetre even, and all the Indians open to British gold and British rum. Then there was another question : Will the people at home sustain us?

At nine o'clock President Hancock rapped to order. The first business was the reading of letters addressed to the Congress, which had arrived since the adjournment on Saturday. One of these, from General Washington in New York, contained news calculated to alarm all but the most stalwart spirits : Canada quite lost to the cause ; Arnold's army in full, though orderly, retreat from that province ; a powerful British fleet just arriving in New York harbor, three or four ships drifting in daily, and now forty-five sail all at once signalled from Sandy Hook.

"Some say more," added General Washington, "and I suppose the whole fleet will be in within a day or two."

The whole fleet! As if these were not enough ; and, in truth, the number soon reached a hundred and twenty, with thousands of red-coats in them abundantly supplied with every requisite. Washington's own army numbered on that day seven thousand seven hundred and fifty-four men, of whom, as he reported, eight hundred had no guns at all, fourteen hundred had bad guns, and half the infantry no bayonets. Add to this fifty-three British ships just arrived at Charleston, with General Clinton's expedition on board.

We must bear this news in mind in order to appreciate what followed in Congress that day. When General Washington's letter had been read, the House went into committee of the whole, "to take into consideration the question of Independence."

The boldest man upon that floor could not avoid feeling that the crisis was serious and the issue doubtful. As if to deepen this impression, there soon rose to address the House John Dickinson, of Pennsylvania, a good man and a patriot, an able speaker and better writer, but rich, not of robust health, and conservative almost to timidity. From the first, while opposing the arbitrary measures of the King, he had been equally opposed to a Declaration of Independence ; and to-day, refreshed by the rest of Sunday, and feeling that it was now or never with his party, he spoke with all the force and solemnity of which he was capable.

"I value," said he, "the love of my country as I ought, but I value my country more, and I desire this illustrious assembly to witness the integrity, if not the policy, of my conduct. The first campaign will be decisive of the controversy.

" The declaration will not strengthen us by one man, or by the least supply, while it may expose our soldiers to additional cruelties and outrages. Without some preliminary trials of our strength we ought not to commit our country upon an alternative where to recede would be infamy, and to persist might be destruction."

In this strain he spoke long, urging all the reasons for delay which an ingenious mind could devise, and clothing his argument with the charm of a fine literary style.

He ceased. There was a pause. No one seemed willing to break the silence, until it began to be embarrassing, and then painful.

Many eyes were turned toward John Adams, who for eighteen months had been the chief spokesman of the party for independence. He had advocated the measure before Thomas Paine had written " Common Sense," and when it had not one influential friend in Philadelphia. Early in the previous year, when it first became known by the accidental publicity of a letter that he favored the Declaration of Independence, the solid men of Philadelphia shunned him as if he had had the leprosy.

"I walked the streets of Philadelphia," he once wrote, "in solitude, borne down by the weight of care and unpopularity," and Dr. Rush mentions that he saw him thus walking the streets alone, "an object of nearly universal scorn and detestation."

But he was on the gaining side. The cruel burning of Falmouth on the coast of Maine weaned New England from the mother country, and the burning of Norfolk completed the same office for Virginia.

To-day he stood with a majority of the people behind him. To-day he spoke the sentiments of his country. To-day he uttered the words which every man on the floor but John Dickinson wished to hear uttered.

Yet he did not immediately rise : for he wished some one else, some one less committed to Independence than he was, to take the lead in that day's debate. At length, however, since every one else hung back, he got upon his feet to answer Mr. Dickinson.

The speech which he delivered on this occasion was deemed by those who heard it the most powerful effort of his life, though he had made no special preparation for it beforehand. He had thought of the subject from his college days, and had never ceased to regard the Independence of his country as only a question of time. During his professional life, it had been the frequent theme of his reflections, and he was perfectly familiar with every phase of it.

"This is the first time in my life," said he, "that I have ever wished for the talents and eloquence of the ancient orators of Greece and Rome, for I am very sure that none of them ever had before him a question of more importance to his country and to the world. They would, probably, upon less occasions than this, have begun by solemn invocations to their divinities for assistance.

"But the question before me appears so simple that I have confidence enough in the plain understanding and common-sense that have been given me to believe that I can answer, to the satisfaction of the House, all the arguments which have been produced, notwithstanding the abilities which have been displayed and the eloquence with which they have been enforced."

Proceeding then to the discussion of the question, he dwelt strongly upon the point that, as the colonies had gone too far to recede, as they had already been put outside of British law, the Declaration of Independence could not possibly make their condition worse, but would give them some obvious and solid advantages.

Now, they were rebels against their king, and could not negotiate on equal terms with a sovereign power. The moment they declared Independence, they would be themselves a sovereignty. The measure, he contended, would be as prudent as it was just. It would help them in many ways and hinder them in no way.

We have no report of this celebrated oration, and can only gather its purport from allusions scattered here and there in the letters of those who heard it. We know, however, that Mr. Adams dwelt forcibly upon this one position, that the king himself having absolved them from their allegiance, and having made unprovoked war upon them, the proposed Declaration would be simply a proclamation to the world of a state of things already existing.

Many members followed. When the debate had proceeded for a long time, three new members from New Jersey came in: Richard Stockton, Dr. Witherspoon and Francis Hopkinson. These gentlemen, on learning the business before the House, expressed a strong desire to hear a recapitulation of the arguments which had been brought forward.

Again there was an awkward silence. Again all eyes were turned upon John Adams. Again he shrank from taking the floor. Mr. Edward Rutledge of South Carolina came to him and said :

" Nobody will speak but you upon this subject. You have all the topics so ready that you must satisfy the gentlemen from New Jersey."

Mr. Adams replied that he was ashamed to repeat what he had said twenty times before. As the new members still insisted on hearing a recapitulation, he at length rose once more, and gave a concise summary of the whole debate. The New Jersey gentlemen said they were fully satisfied and were ready for the question. It was now six o'clock in the evening. The debate had continued all day, nine hours, without the least interval for rest or refeshment, and during that long period, as Mr. Jefferson wrote at a later day, "all the powers of the soul had been distended with the magnitude of the object."

Mr. Edward Rutledge, of South Carolina, then rose, and asked as a favor that the voting be deferred until the next morning, as he and his fellow-members wished still further to deliberate.

The request was granted ; the House adjourned ; the hungry and exhausted members went to their homes.

The next morning members met in a cheerful mood, for it was well ascertained that every colony was prepared to vote for Independence. When Mr. Adams reached the State House door, he had the pleasure of meeting Cæsar Rodney, still in his riding-boots, for he had ridden all night from Delaware to vote on the momentous question. Mr. Adams, it is said, had sent an express at his own expense eighty miles to summon him, and there he was to greet him at the State House door.

The great question was speedily put, when every State but New York voted for declaring independence, and that State's adherence was delayed a few days only by a series of accidents.

What a happy man was John Adams, and what a triumphant letter was that which he wrote to his noble wife on the 3d of July, telling her the great news that Congress had passed a resolution, without one dissenting colony, "that these united colonies are, and of right ought to be, free and independent States." Then he continued in the passage so often quoted:

"The second day of July, 1776, will be the most memorable epoch in the history of America. I am apt to believe that it will be celebrated by succeeding generations as the great anniversary festival. It ought to be commemorated as the day of deliverance by solemn acts of devotion to God Almighty. It ought to be solemnized with pomp and parade, with shows, games, sports, guns, bells, bonfires and illuminations from one end of this continent to the other, from this time forward forevermore."

But, no; not on July second. The transaction was not yet complete. As soon as the vote was recorded, Mr. Jefferson's draft of the Declaration was taken from the table, and discussed paragraph by paragraph. Many alterations were made, thirty four in all, most of them for the better. This discussion lasted the rest of that day, all the next, and most of the next, which was the fourth. Late in that afternoon the members present signed the document, and so the day we celebrate is the FOURTH OF JULY.

ANECDOTES OF JOHN ADAMS.

THE first office ever held by President John Adams was that of Roadmaster to his native town. The young barris-ter, as he himself confesses, was very indignant at being elected to a post, with the duties of which he was unac-quainted, and which he considered beneath his pretensions. His friend, Dr. Savil, explained to him that he had nomi-nated him to the office to prevent his being elected con-stable.

"They make it a rule," said the Doctor, "to compel every man to serve either as constable or surveyor of the highways, or to pay a fine."

"They might as well," said Mr. Adams, "have chosen any boy in school, for I know nothing of the business; but since they have chosen me at a venture, I will accept it in the same manner, and find out my duty as I can."

Accordingly he went to plowing, ditching, and blowing rocks and built a new stone bridge over a stream. He took infinite pains with his bridge, and employed the best work-men; "but," says he, "the next spring brought down a flood that threw my bridge all into ruins." The blame, how-ever, fell upon the workmen, and all the town, he tells us, agreed that he had executed his office with "impartiality, diligence, and spirit."

Mr. Adams was an extremely passionate man. One evening, just before the breaking out of the Revolution, while spending an evening in company with an English gen-tleman, the conversation turned upon the aggressions of the mother country. He became furious with anger. He said there was no justice left in Britain; that he wished for war, and that the whole Bourbon family was upon the back of Great Britain. He wished that anything might happen to them, and, as the clergy prayed for enemies in time of war, that " they might be brought to reason or to ruin." When he went home he was exceedingly repentant for having lost his temper, and wrote in his diary the following remarks:

" I cannot but reflect upon myself with severity for these rash, inexperienced, boyish, wrong, and awkward expressions. A man who has no better government of his tongue, no more command of his temper, is unfit for anything but children's play, and the company of boys. A character can never be supported, if it can be raised, without a good, a great share of self-government. Such flights of passion, such starts of imagination, though they may strike a few of the fiery and inconsiderate, yet they sink a man with the wise. They expose him to danger, as well as familiarity, contempt, and ridicule."

One of the most interesting events in the life of John Adams was his nomination of George Washington to the command of the Revolutionary armies. One day, in 1775, when Congress was full of anxiety concerning the army near Boston, and yet hesitated to adopt it as their own, fearing to take so decisive a step, John and Samuel Adams were walking up and down the State House yard in Philadelphia before the opening of the session, and were conversing upon the situation.

" What shall we do?" asked Samuel Adams, at length.

His kinsman said: " You know I have taken great pains to get our colleagues to agree upon *some* plan that we might be unanimous upon ; but you know they will pledge themselves to nothing ; but I am determined to take a step which shall compel them, and all the other members of Congress, to declare themselves for or against *something*. I am determined this morning to make a direct motion that Congress shall adopt the army before Boston, and appoint Colonel Washington commander of it."

Samuel Adams looked grave at this proposition, but said nothing. When Congress had assembled, John Adams rose, and, in a short speech, represented the state of the colonies, the uncertainty in the minds of the people, the distresses of the army, the danger of its disbanding, the difficulty of collecting another if it should disband, and the probability that the British army would take advantage of our delays, march out of Boston, and spread desolation as far as they could go. He concluded by moving that Congress adopt the army at Cambridge and appoint a general.

"Although," he continued, "this is not the proper time to nominate a general, yet, as I have reason to believe that this is a point of the greatest difficulty, I have no hesitation to declare that I have but one gentleman in my mind for that important command, and that is a gentleman from Virginia, who is among us, and is very well known to all of us; a gentleman whose skill and experience as an officer, whose independent fortune, great talents, and excellent universal character will command the approbation of all America, and unite the cordial exertions of all the colonies better than any other person in the Union."

When Mr. Adams began this speech, Colonel Washington was present; but as soon as the orator pronounced the words "Gentleman from Virginia," he darted through the nearest door into the library. Mr. Samuel Adams seconded the motion which, as we all know, was, on a future day, unanimously carried. Mr. Adams relates that no one was so displeased with this appointment as John Hancock, the President of Congress.

"While I was speaking," says John Adams, "on the state of the colonies, he heard me with visible pleasure; but when I came to describe Washington for the commander, I never remarked a more sudden and striking change of countenance.

Mortification and resentment were expressed as forcibly as his face could exhibit them."

Hancock, in fact, who was somewhat noted as a militia officer in Massachusetts, was vain enough to aspire to the command of the colonial forces.

They had a fashion, during the Revolutionary war, John Adams tells us, of turning pictures of George III. upside down in the houses of patriots. Adams copied into his diary some lines which were written "under one of these topsey-turvey kings":

> Behold the man who had it in his power
> To make a kingdom tremble and adore.
> Intoxicate with folly, see his head
> Placed where the meanest of his subjects tread.
> Like Lucifer the giddy tyrant fell,
> He lifts his heel to Heaven, but points his head to Hell.

It is evident, from more than one passage in the diary of John Adams, that he, too, in his heart, turned against Gen Washington during the gloomy hours of the Revolution. At least he thought him unfit for the command. Just before the surrender of Burgoyne, Adams wrote in his diary the following passage:

"Gates seems to be acting the same timorous, defensive part which has involved us in so many disasters. Oh, Heaven grant us one great soul! One leading mind would extricate the best cause from that ruin which seems to await it for the want of it. We have as good a cause as ever was fought for; we have great resources; the people are well tempered; one active, masterly capacity would bring order out of this confusion, and save this country."

Thus it is always in war-time. When the prospect is gloomy, and when disasters threaten to succeed disasters, there is a general distrust of the general in command, though at that very time he may be exhibiting greater qualities and greater talents than ever before.

John Adams tells us the reason why Thomas Jefferson, out of a committee of five, was chosen to write the Declaration of Independence.

" Writings of his," says Mr. Adams, " were handed about, remarkable for the peculiar felicity of expression. Though a silent member in Congress, he was so frank, explicit and decisive upon committees and in conversation (not even Samuel Adams was more so) that he soon seized upon my heart ; and upon this occasion I gave him my vote, and did all in my power to procure the votes of others. I think he had one more vote than any other, and that placed him at the head of the committee. I had the next highest number, and that placed me the second. The committee met, discussed the subject, and then appointed Mr. Jefferson and me to make the draft, because we were the two first upon the list."

When this sub-committee of two had their first meeting, Jefferson urged Mr. Adams to make the draft ; whereupon the following conversation occurred between them :

" I will not," said Mr. Adams.

" You should do it," said Jefferson.

" Oh no," repeated Adams.

" Why will you not ?" asked Jefferson. " You ought to do it."

" I will not," rejoined Adams.

" Why ?" again asked Jefferson.

" Reasons enough," said Adams.

" What can be your reasons ?" inquired Jefferson.

" Reason first—you are a Virginian, and a Virginian ought to appear at the head of this business. Reason second—I am obnoxious, suspected, and unpopular. You are very much otherwise. Reason third—you can write ten-times better than I can."

"Well," said Jefferson, "if you are decided, I will do as well as I can."

"Very well," said Mr. Adams; "when you have drawn it up, we will have a meeting."

Thus it was that Thomas Jefferson became the author of this celebrated document. Mr. Adams informs us that the original draft contained "a vehement philippic against negro slavery," which Congress ordered to be stricken out.

Mr. Adams relates an amusing story of his sleeping one night with Doctor Franklin, when they were on their way to hold their celebrated conference with Lord Howe on Staten Island. It was at Brunswick, in New Jersey, where the tavern was so crowded that two of the commissioners were put into one room, which was little larger than the bed, and which had no chimney and but one small window. The window was open when the two members went up to bed, which Mr. Adams seeing, and being afraid of the night air, shut it close.

"Oh," said Doctor Franklin, "don't shut the window, we shall be suffocated."

Mr. Adams answered that he was afraid of the evening air; to which Doctor Franklin replied:

"The air within this chamber will soon be, and indeed is now, worse than that without doors. Come, open the window and come to bed, and I will convince you. I believe you are not acquainted with my theory of colds."

Mr. Adams complied with both these requests. He tells us that when he was in bed, the Doctor began to harangue upon air, and cold, and respiration, and perspiration, with which he was so much amused that he soon fell asleep. It does not appear that any ill consequences followed from their breathing during the night the pure air of heaven.

The Writing and Signing of the Declaration of Independence.

We happen to know what kind of weather it was in Philadelphia on Thursday, the Fourth of July, 1776. Mr. Jefferson was in the habit, all his life, of recording the temperature three times a day, and not unfrequently four times. He made four entries in his weather record on this birthday of the nation, as if anticipating that posterity would be curious to learn every particular of an occasion so interesting. At six that morning the mercury marked sixty-eight degrees. At nine, just before going round to the State House to attend the session of Congress, he recorded seventy-two and a half degrees. At one, while he was at home during the recess for dinner, he found the mercury at seventy-six. At nine in the evening, when the great deed had been done, the instrument indicated seventy-three and a half degrees.

From another entry of Mr. Jefferson's we learn that he paid for a new thermometer on that day. The following are the three entries in his expense-book for July fourth, 1776:

"Paid Sparhawk for a thermometer.................£3 15s.
Pd. for 7 pr. women's gloves......................... 27s.
Gave in charity............................. .... 1s. 6d."

The price that he paid for his thermometer was equivalent to about twenty dollars in gold; and as Mr. Jefferson was not likely to spend his money for an elaborately decorated thermometer, we may infer that instruments of that nature were at least ten times as costly then as they are now. An excellent standard thermometer at the present time can be bought for five dollars, and the sum which Mr. Jefferson paid in 1776 was fully equal, in purchasing power, to fifty dollars in our present currency.

Mr. Jefferson lived then on the south side of Market street, not far from the corner of Seventh, in Philadelphia. As it was the only house then standing in that part of the street, he was unable in after years to designate the exact spot, though he was always under the impression that it was a corner house, either on the corner of Seventh street or very near it. The owner of the house, named Graaf, was a young man, the son of a German, and then newly married. Soon after coming to Philadelphia, Mr. Jefferson hired the whole of the second floor, ready furnished; and as the floor consisted of but two rooms—a parlor and a bed-room—we may conjecture that the house was of no great size. It was in that parlor that he wrote the Declaration of Independence.

The writing-desk upon which he wrote it exists in Boston, and is still possessed by the venerable friend and connection of Mr. Jefferson to whom he gave it. The note which the author of the Declaration wrote when he sent this writing-desk to the husband of one of his grand-daughters, has a particular interest for us at this present time. It was written in 1825, nearly fifty years after the Declaration was signed, about midway between that glorious period and the Centennial. It is as follows :

"Thomas Jefferson gives this writing-desk to Joseph Coolidge, Jr., as a memorial of affection. It was made from a drawing of his own by Benj. Randolph, cabinet-maker, at Philadelphia, with whom he first lodged on his arrival in that city, in May, 1776, and is the identical one on which he wrote the Declaration of Independence. Politics as well as religion has its superstitions. These, gaining strength with time, may one day give imaginary value to this relic for its associations with the birth of the Great charter of our Independence."

The note given above, although penned when Mr. Jefferson was eighty-two years of age, is written in a small, firm hand, and is quite as legible as the type which the reader is now perusing. There is no indication of old age in the writing; but I observe that he has spelt the most important word of the note French fashion, thus: "*Indcpendancc*." It certainly is remarkable that the author of the Declaration of Independence should have made a mistake in spelling the word. Nor can it be said that the erroneous letter was a slip of the pen, because the word occurs twice in the note, and both times the last syllable is spelt with an *a*. Mr. Jefferson was a very exact man, and yet, like most men of that day, he used capitals and omitted them with an apparent carelessness. In the above note, for example, the following words occur, "Great charter." Here he furnishes the adjective with a capital, and reduces his noun to the insignificance of a small letter.

The Declaration was written, I suppose, about the middle of June; and, while he was writing it, Philadelphia was all astir with warlike preparation. Seldom has a peaceful city, a city of Quakers and brotherly love, undergone such a transformation as Philadelphia did in a few months. As Mr. Jefferson sat at his little desk composing the Declaration, with the windows open at that warm season, he must have heard the troops drilling in Independence Square. Twice a day they were out drilling, to the number of two thousand men, and more. Perhaps he was looking out of the window on the eleventh of June, the very day after the appointment of the committee to draw up the Declaration, when the question of independence was voted upon by the whole body of Philadelphia volunteers, and they all voted for independence except twenty-nine men, four officers and twenty-five privates. One of these objectors made a scene upon the parade. He was so much opposed to the proceeding that he would not put the question to his company. This refusal, said the newspaper of that week, "Gave great umbrage to the men, one of whom replied to him in a genteel and spirited manner.

Besides this morning and afternoon drill in the public squares of the town, preparations were going forward to close the river against the ascent of a hostile fleet. Dr. Franklin, as I have related, had twenty or thirty row galleys in readiness, which were out on the river practising every day, watched by approving groups on the shore. Men were at work on the forts five miles below the city, where, also, Dr. Franklin was arranging his three rows of iron-barbed beams in the channel, which were called *chevaux de frise.* In a letter of that day, written to Captain Richard Varick, of New York, I find these French words spelt thus: "Shiver de freeses." Committees were going about Philadelphia during this spring buying lead from house to house at sixpence a pound, taking even the lead clock-weights and giving iron ones in exchange. So destitute was the army of powder and ball that Dr. Franklin seriously proposed arming some regiments with javelins and crossbows.

Mr. Jefferson was ready with his draft in time to present it to Congress on the first of July; but it was on the second, as I conjecture, that the great debate occurred upon it, when the timid men again put forward the argument that the country was not yet ripe for so decisive a measure. Mr. Dickinson, of Pennsylvania, a true patriot, but a most timorous and conservative gentleman, who had opposed Independence from the beginning, delivered a long and eloquent speech against the measure.

The author of the Declaration used to relate after dinner to his guests at Monticello, that the conclusion of the business was hastened by a ridiculous cause. Near the hall was a livery stable, from which swarms of flies came in at the open windows, and attacked the trouserless legs of members, who wore the silk stockings of the period. Lashing the flies with their handkerchiefs, they became at length unable to bear a longer delay, and the decisive vote was taken. On the Monday following, in the presence of a great crowd of people assembled in Independence Square, it was read by Captain Ezekiel Hopkins, the first commodore of the American Navy, then just home from a cruise, during which he had captured eighty cannon, a large quantity of ammunition, and stores, and two British vessels. He was selected to read the Declaration from the remarkable power of his voice. Seven weeks later, the Declaration was engrossed upon parchment, which was signed by the members, and which now hangs in the Patent Office at Washington.

Robert Morris,

The Financier of the Revolution.

Robert Morris, who had charge of the financial affairs of the thirteen States during the Revolutionary War, and afterwards extended his business beyond that of any other person in the country, became bankrupt at last, spent four years of his old age in a debtor's prison, and owed his subsistance, during his last illness, to a small annuity rescued by his wife from the wreck of their fortunes.

Morris was English by birth, a native of Lancashire, where he lived until he was thirteen years of age. Emigrating to Philadelphia in 1747, he was placed in the counting-house of one of the leading merchants, with whose son he entered into partnership before he had completed his twenty-first year. This young firm, Willing, Morris & Co., embarked boldly and ably in commerce, until at the beginning of the Revolution it was the wealthiest commercial firm in the Colonies south of New England, and only surpassed in New England by two. When the contention arose between the Mother country and the colonies, his interest was to take the side of the Mother country. But he sided with the Colonies—to the great detriment of his private business. He served in Congress during nearly the whole of the War, and was almost constantly employed in a struggle with the financial difficulties of the situation.

I do not see how the revolution could have been maintained unless some such person could have been found to undertake the finances. When all other resources gave out he never refused to employ his private resources, as well as the immense, unquestioned credit of his firm, in aid of the cause. On several occasions he borrowed money for the use of the government, pledging all his estate for the re payment. In 1780, aided by the powerful pen of Thomas Paine, he established a bank through which three million rations were provided for the army. Fortunately, he was reputed to be much richer than he was, and thus he was several times enabled to furnish an amount of assistance far beyond the resources of any private individual then living in America.

His greatest achievement was in assisting General Washington in 1781 to transport his army to Virginia, and to maintain it there during the operations against Lord Cornwallis. In the spring of that year the revolution appeared to be all but exhausted. The treasury was not merely empty, but there was a floating debt upon it of two millions and a half, and the soldiers were clamorous for their pay. The Superintendent of Finance rose to the occasion. He issued his own notes to the amount of fourteen hundred thousand dollars by which the army was supplied with pro visions and the campaign carried on to the middle of August.

Then General Washington, in confidence, revealed to Robert Morris his intention to transport his army to Virginia. To effect this operation the general required all the light vessels of the Delaware and Chesapeake, six hundred barrels of provisions for the march, a vast supply in Virginia, five hundred guineas in gold for secret service, and a month's pay in silver for the army. When this information reached the superintendent he was already at his wits' end, and really supposed that he had exhausted every resource.

"I am sorry to inform you," he wrote to the general, "that I find money-matters in as bad a situation as possible."

And he mentions in his diary of the same date that, during a recent visit to camp, he had had with him one hundred and fifty guineas; but so many officers came to him with claims upon the government, that he thought it best to satisfy none, and brought the money home again. After unheard-of exertions, he contrived to get together provisions and vessels for the transportation. But to raise the hard money to comply with General Washington's urgent request for a month's pay for the troops, was beyond his power. At the last moment he laid the case before the French admiral, and borrowed for a few weeks from the fleet treasury twenty thousand silver dollars. Just in the nick of time, Colonel Laurens arrived from France with five hundred thousand dollars in cash, which enabled Morris to pay this debt, and to give General Washington far more efficient support than he had hoped.

To Robert Morris we owe one of the most pleasing accounts of the manner in which the surrender of Cornwallis was celebrated at Philadelphia. He records that on the third of November, 1781, on the invitation of the French Minister, he attended the Catholic Church, where *Te Deum* was sung in acknowledgment of the victory. Soon after, all the flags captured from the enemy were brought to

Philadelphia by two of General Washington's aids, the city troop of Light Horse going out to meet them several miles. The flags were twenty-four in number, and each of them was carried into the city by one of the light horsemen. Morris concludes his account of this great day with affecting simplicity:

" The American and French flags preceded the captured trophies, which were conducted to the State House, where they were presented to Congress, who were sitting; and many of the members tell me, that instead of viewing the transaction as a mere matter of joyful ceremony, which they expected to do, they instantly felt themselves impressed with ideas of the most solemn nature. It brought to their minds the distresses our country has been exposed to, the calamities we have repeatedly suffered, the perilous situations which our affairs have almost always been in; and they could not but recollect the threats of Lord North that he would bring America to his feet on unconditional terms of submission."

When the war was over, the finances of the country did not improve. In conjunction with General Washington and Robert R. Livingston, Secretary of Foreign Affairs, he hit upon a plan to recall the State legislatures to a sense of their duty. He engaged Thomas Paine, at a salary of eight hundred dollars a year, to employ his pen in reconciling the people to the necessity of supporting the burden of taxation, in setting forth, in his eloquent manner, the bravery and good conduct of the soldiers whose pay was so terribly in arrears, and in convincing the people of the need of a stronger confederated government.

" It was also agreed," says Morris in his private diary, " that this allowance should not be known to any other persons except General Washington, Mr. Livingston, Gouverneur Morris, and myself, lest the publications might lose their force if it were known that the author is paid for them by government."

The expedient did not suffice. The States were backward in voting contributions, and, in 1784, Robert Morris resigned his office after discharging all his personal obligations incurred on account of the Government. He then resumed his private business. He was the first American citizen who ever sent to Canton an American vessel. This was in 1784, and he continued for many years to carry on an extensive commerce with India and China.

Unhappily, in his old age, for some cause or causes that have never been recorded, he lost his judgment as a business man. About 1791, he formed a land company, which bought from the Six Nations in the State of New York a tract of land equal in extent to several of the German Principalities of that time, and they owned some millions of acres in five other States. These lands, bought for a trifling sum, would have enriched every member of the company if they had not omitted from their calculations the important element of *time*. But a gentleman sixty years of age cannot wait twenty years for the development of a speculation. Confident in the soundness of his calculations and expecting to be speedily rich beyond the dreams of avarice, he erected in Philadelphia a palace for his own abode, of the most preposterous magnificence. The architect assured him that the building would cost sixty thousand dollars, but the mere cellars exhausted that sum. He imported from Europe the most costly furniture and fine statuary for this house.

But ardent speculators do not take into consideration the obvious and certain truth that no country enjoys a long period of buoyancy in money affairs. Hamilton's financial schemes led to such a sudden increase of values as to bring on a period of the wildest speculation; which was followed, as it always is, by reaction and collapse. Then came the threatened renewal of the war with Great Britain, followed by the long imbroglio with France, which put a stop to emigration for years. The Western lands did not sell. The bubble burst. Robert Morris was ruined. He was arrested in 1797 upon the suit of one Blair McClenachan, to whom he owed sixteen thousand dollars, and he was confined in the debtors' prison in Philadelphia, as before mentioned, for four years. Nor would he have ever been released but for the operation of a new bankrupt law. A paragraph from one of his letters, written when he had been in prison two weeks, few people can read without emotion. These are the words of a man who had been a capitalist and lived in luxury more than forty years:

" I have tried in vain," he wrote, " to get a room exclusively to myself, and hope to be able to do so in a few days, but at a high rent which I am unable to bear. Then I may set up a bed in it, and have a chair or two and a table, and so be made comfortable. Now I am very uncomfortable, for I have no particular place allotted me. I feel like an intruder everywhere ; sleeping in other people's beds, and sitting in other people's rooms. I am writing on other people's paper with other people's ink. The pen is my own. That and the clothes I wear are all that I can claim as mine here."

Released in 1802, he lived with his wife in a small house on the outskirts of the city, where he died in 1806 aged seventy-two.

It was often proposed in Congress to appropriate some of the money belonging to the industrious and frugal people of the United States to pay the debts of this rash speculator ; and many writers since have censured the government for not doing something for his relief. The simple and sufficient answer is, that Congress has no constitutional power to apply the people's money to any such purpose. The government holds the public treasure *in trust*. It is a trustee, not a proprietor. It can spend public money only for purposes which the constitution specifies; and, among these specified purposes, we do *not* find the relief of land speculators who build gorgeous palaces on credit.

John Jay,

The First Chief-Justice.

It was the tyranny of Louis XIV., King of France, that drove the ancestor of John Jay to America. Pierre Jay, two hundred years ago, was a rich merchant in the French city of Rochelle. He was a Protestant—one of those worthy Frenchmen whom the revocation of the Edict of Nantes expelled from the country of which they were the most valuable inhabitants. In 1685, the Protestant Church which he attended at Rochelle was demolished, and dragoons were quartered in the houses of its members. Secretly getting his family and a portion of his property on board of a ship, he sent them to England, and contrived soon after in a ship of his own, laden with a valuable cargo, to escape himself.

It was not, however, from Pierre Jay that our American Jays were immediately descended, but from Augustus, one of his sons. It so happened that Augustus Jay, at the time of his father's flight, was absent from France on a mercantile mission to Africa, and he was astonished on returning to Rochelle to find himself without home or family. Nor was he free from the danger of arrest unless he changed his religion. Assisted by some friends, he took passage in a ship bound to Charleston in South Carolina which he reached in safety about the year 1686. Finding the climate of South

Carolina injurious to his health, he removed to New York, near which there was a whole village of refugees from his native city, which they had named New Rochelle, a village which has since grown to a considerable town, with which all New Yorkers are acquainted. His first employment here was that of supercargo, which he continued to exercise for several years, and in which he attained a moderate prosperity.

In 1697 Augustus Jay married Ann Maria Bayard, the daughter of a distinguished Dutch family, who assisted him into business, and greatly promoted his fortunes. The only son of this marriage was Peter Jay, who, in his turn, married Mary Van Cortlandt, the child of another of the leading Dutch families of the city. This Peter Jay had ten children of whom John, the subject of this article, was the eighth, born in New York in 1745. In him were therefore united the vivacious blood of France with the solid qualities of the Dutch; and, accordingly, we find in him something of the liveliness of the French along with a great deal of Dutch prudence and caution.

After graduating from King's College,* John Jay became a law student in the city of New York, in the office of Benjamin Kissam—still a well-known New York name. An anecdote related of this period reveals the French side of his character. He asked his father to allow him to keep a saddle horse in the city, a request with which the prudent father hesitated to comply.

" Horses," said he, "are not very good companions for a young man ; and John, why do you want a horse ?"

" That I may have the means, sir," adroitly replied the son, " of visiting you frequently."

The father was vanquished, gave him a horse, and was rewarded by receiving a visit from his son at his country

* Now Columbia.

house in Rye, twenty-five miles from the city, every other week.

Another anecdote betrays the Frenchman. Soon after his admission to the bar, being opposed in a suit to Mr. Kissam, his preceptor, he somewhat puzzled and embarrassed that gentleman in the course of his argument. Alluding to this, Mr. Kissam pleasantly said:

" I see, your honor, that I have brought up a bird to pick out my own eyes."

" Oh, no," instantly replied Mr. Jay; " not to pick out, but to open your eyes."

Inheriting a large estate, and being allied either by marriage or by blood with most of the powerful families of the province, and being himself a man of good talents and most respectable character, he made rapid advance in his profession, and gained a high place in the esteem and confidence of his fellow-citizens ; so that when the first Congress met at Philadelphia, in 1774, John Jay was one of those who represented in it the colony of New York. He was then twenty-nine years of age, and was, perhaps, the youngest member of the body, every individual of which he outlived.

Some of the best written papers of that session were of his composition. It was he who wrote that memorable address to the people of Great Britain, in which the wrongs of the colonists were expressed with so much eloquence, conciseness, and power. He left his lodgings in Philadelphia, it is said, and shut himself up in a room in a tavern to secure himself from interruption, and there penned the address which was the foundation of his political fortunes.

At an early period of the Revolution he was appointed Minister to Spain, where he struggled with more persistance than success to induce a timid and dilatory government to render some substantial aid to his country. He was afterwards one of the commissioners who negotiated the treaty with Great Britain, in which the independence of the United States was acknowledged, and its boundaries settled. Soon after his return home Congress appointed him Secretary for Foreign Affairs, which was the most important office in their gift, and in which he displayed great ability in the dispatch of business.

Like all the great men of that day—like Washington, Jefferson, Franklin, Hamilton, Patrick Henry, John Randolph, and all others of similar grade—John Jay was an ardent abolitionist. He brought home with him from abroad one negro slave, to whom he gave his freedom when he had served long enough to repay him the expense incurred in bringing him to America.

Mr. Jay, upon the division of the country into Republicans and Federalists, became a decided Federalist, and took a leading part in the direction of that great party. President Washington appointed him Chief-Justice of the Supreme Court, an office which he soon resigned. The most noted of all his public services was the negotiation of a treaty with Great Britain in 1794. The terms of this treaty were revolting in the extreme, both to the pride of Americans and to their sense of justice; and Mr. Jay was overwhelmed with the bitterest reproaches from the party opposed to his own. No man, however, has ever been able to show that better terms were attainable; nor can any candid person now hold the opinion that the United States should have preferred war to the acceptance of those terms. If a very skillful negotiator could have done somewhat better for his country, Mr. Jay did the best he could, and, probably, as well as any man could have done.

Never was a public man more outrageously abused. On one occasion, a mob paraded the streets of Philadelphia, carrying an image of Mr. Jay holding a pair of scales. One of the scales was labeled, "American Liberty and Independence," and the other, "British Gold," the latter weighing down the former as low as it could go, while from the mouth of the effigy issued the words:

"Come up to my price and I will sell you my country."

The effigy was finally burnt in one of the public squares.

Notwithstanding this storm of abuse, Mr. Jay was elected Governor of New York, from which office he retired to his pleasant seat at Bedford, where he spent the remainder of his life. He lived to the year 1829, when he died, aged eighty-four years, leaving children and grandchildren who have sustained his high character, illustrated his memory, and continued his work.

FISHER AMES,

THE ORATOR OF THE FOURTH CONGRESS.

AND who was Fisher Ames, that his "Speeches" should be gathered and re-published sixty-three years after his death? He was a personage in his time. Let us look upon him in the day of his greatest glory.

It was April 28, 1796, at Philadelphia, in the Hall of the House of Representatives, of which Fisher Ames was a member. The House and country were highly excited respecting the terms of the treaty which John Jay had negotiated with the British government. To a large number of the people this treaty was inexpressibly odious; as, indeed, *any* treaty would have been with a power so abhorred by them as England then was. Some of the conditions of the treaty, we cannot deny, were hard, unwise, unjust; but, in all probability, it was the best that could then have been obtained, and Mr. Jay had only the alternative of accepting the conditions, or plunging his country into war. One great point,

at least, the British government had yielded.   After the
Revolutionary war, the English had retained several western
posts, to the great annoyance of settlers, and the indignation
of the whole country.   These posts were now to be surrendered, provided the treaty was accepted and its conditions
fulfilled.

President Washington and the Senate had ratified the
treaty—with reluctance, it is true; but still they had ratified
it; and nothing remained but for the House of Representatives to appropriate the money requisite for carrying the
treaty into effect.   But here was the difficulty.   The treaty
was so unpopular that members of Congress shrunk from
even seeming to approve it.   There had been riotous meet-
ings in all the large cities to denounce it.   In New York,
Alexander Hamilton, while attempting to address a meeting
in support of it, was pelted with stones, and the people then
marched to the residence of Mr. Jay, and burned a copy of
the treaty before his door.

"Blush," said a Democratic editor, "to think that
America should degrade herself so much as to enter into
any kind of treaty with a power now tottering on the brink
of ruin, whose principles are directly contrary to the spirit
of Republicanism!"

A Virginia newspaper advised that, if the treaty negotiated by "that arch-traitor, John Jay, with the British
tyrant, should be ratified," Virginia should secede from the
Union.   Indeed, the public mind has seldom been excited
to such a degree upon any public topic.

It was in these circumstances that Fisher Ames rose to
address the House of Representatives, in favor of the treaty.
There was supposed to be a majority of ten against it in the
House, and the debate had been for some days in progress.
Madison and all the leading Democrats had spoken strongly
against it; while Fisher Ames, the greatest orator on the

side of the Administration, was suffering from the pulmonary disease from which he afterward died, and had been ordered by his physician not to speak a word in the House. Inaction at such a time became insupportable to him, and he chafed under it day after day.

"I am like an old gun," he wrote, in one of his letters, "that is spiked, or the trunnions knocked off, and yet am carted off, not for the worth of the old iron, but to balk the enemy of a trophy. My political life is ended, and I am the survivor of myself; or, rather, a troubled ghost of a politician that am condemned to haunt the field where he fell."

But as the debate went on, he could no longer endure to remain silent. He determined to speak, if he never spoke again; and the announcement of his intention filled the Representatives' Chamber with a brilliant assembly of ladies and gentlemen. Vice-President Adams came to the chamber to hear him, among other persons of note. The orator rose from his seat pale, feeble, scarcely able to stand, or to make himself heard; but as he proceeded he gathered strength, and was able to speak for nearly two hours in a strain of eloquence, the tradition of which fills a great place in the memoirs of the time. The report of it which we possess is imperfect, and the reading of it is somewhat disappointing; but here and there there is a passage in the report which gives us some notion of the orator's power. One of his points was, that the faith of the country had been pledged by the ratification of the treaty, and that consequently a refusal of the House to appropriate the money would be a breach of faith. This led him to expatiate upon the necessity of national honor.

"In Algiers," said he, "a truce may be bought for money; but when ratified, even Algiers is too wise or too just to disown and annul its obligation. . . . If there could be a resurrection from the foot of the gallows; if the victims of justice could live again, collect together and form a society, they would, however loath, soon find themselves obliged to make justice—that justice under which they fell—the fundamental law of their State."

This speech was afterward called Fisher Ames' Tomahawk Speech, because he endeavored to show that, if the posts were not surrendered and not garrisoned by American troops, the Indians could not be kept in check, and would fill the frontier with massacre and fire.

"On this theme," the orator exclaimed, "my emotions are unutterable. If I could find words for them, if my powers bore any proportion to my zeal, I would swell my voice to such a note of remonstrance, it should reach every log-house beyond the mountains. I would say to the inhabitants, Wake from your false security! Your cruel dangers, your more cruel apprehensions, are soon to be renewed; the wounds yet unhealed are to be torn open again; in the daytime your path through the woods will be ambushed; the darkness of midnight will glitter with the blaze of your dwellings. You are a father—the blood of your sons shall fatten your corn-fields. You are a mother—the war-whoop shall wake the sleep of the cradle."

He continued in this strain for some time, occasionally blazing into a simile that delighted every hearer with its brilliancy, while flashing a vivid light upon the subject; and I only wish the space at my command permitted further extracts. The conclusion of the speech recalled attention to the orator's feeble condition of health, which the vigor of his speech might have made his hearers forget.

"I have, perhaps," said he, "as little personal interest in the event as any one here. There is, I believe, no member who will not think his chance to be a witness of the consequences greater than mine. If, however, the vote should pass to reject, and a spirit should arise, as it will, with the public disorders, to make confusion worse confounded, even I, slender and almost broken as my hold upon life is, may outlive the government and constitution of my country."

With these words the orator resumed his seat. The great assembly seemed spell-bound, and some seconds elapsed before the buzz of conversation was heard. John Adams turned to a friend, Judge Iredell, who happened to sit next to him, as if looking for sympathy in his own intense admiration.

" My God!" exclaimed the Judge, "how great he is—how great he has been!"

" Noble!" said the Vice-President.

" Bless my stars!" resumed Judge Iredell, " I never heard anything so great since I was born."

" Divine!" exclaimed Adams.

And thus they went on with their interjections, while tears glistened in their eyes. Mr. Adams records that tears enough were shed on the occasion.

" Not a dry eye in the house," he says, " except some of the jackasses who had occasioned the oratory. . . . The ladies wished his soul had a better body."

After many days' further debate, the House voted the money by a considerable majority; a large number of Democrats voting with the administration. Fisher Ames was not so near his death as he supposed, for he lived twelve years after the delivery of this speech, so slow was the progress of his disease. He outlived Washington and Hamilton, and delivered eloquent addresses in commemoration of both.

The great misfortune of his life was that very ill-health to which he alluded in his speech. This tinged his mind with gloom, and caused him to anticipate the future of his country with morbid apprehension. When Jefferson was elected President in 1800, he thought the ruin of his country was sure, and spoke of the " chains" which Jefferson had forged for the people. When Hamilton died, in 1804, he declared that his "soul stiffened with despair," and he compared the fallen statesman to "Hercules treacherously slain in the midst of his unfinished labors, leaving the world overrun with monsters." He was one of the most honest and patriotic of men ; but he had little faith in the truths upon which the Constitution of his country was founded.

He died at his birthplace, Dedham, Massachusetts, on the 4th of July, 1808, in the fifty-first year of his age. His father had been the physician of that place for many years —a man of great skill in his profession, and gifted with a vigorous mind. Doctor Ames died when his son was only six years of age, and it cost the boy a severe and long struggle to work his way through college to the profession of the law, and to public life. If he had had a body equal to his mind, he would have been one of the greatest men New England ever produced.

THE PINCKNEYS OF SOUTH CAROLINA.

In the political writings of Washington's day, we frequently meet with the name of Pinckney ; and, as there were several persons of that name in public life, readers of history are often at a loss to distinguish between them. This confusion is the more troublesome, because they were all of the same family and State, and their career also had a strong family likeness.

The founder of this family in America was Thomas Pinckney, who emigrated to South Carolina in the year 1692. He possessed a large fortune, and built in Charleston a stately mansion, which is still standing, unless it was demolished during the late war. A curious anecdote is related of this original Pinckney, which is about all that is now known of him. Standing at the window of his house one day, with his wife at his side, he noticed a stream of passengers walking up the street, who had just landed from a vessel that day arrived from the West Indies. As they walked along the street, he noticed particularly a handsome man who was very gayly dressed ; and turning to his wife he said :

" That handsome West Indian will marry some poor fellow's widow, break her heart, and ruin her children."

Strange to relate, the widow whom this handsome West Indian married was no other than Mrs. Pinckney herself ; for Thomas Pinckney soon after died, and his widow married the West Indian. He did not break her heart, since she lived to marry a third husband, but he was an extravagant fellow, and wasted part of her children's inheritance. Thomas Pinckney, then, is to be distinguished from others of the name as the *founder* of the family in America.

The eldest son of Thomas, that grew to man's estate, was Charles Pinckney, who embraced the legal profession, and rose to be Chief Justice of the Province of South Carolina, and hence he is usually spoken of and distinguished from the rest of the family as " Chief Justice Pinckney." He was educated in England, and was married there. Returning to Charleston, he acquired a large fortune by the practice of his profession. A strange anecdote is related of his wife also. After he had been married many years without having children, there came to Charleston from England, on a visit of pleasure a young lady named Eliza Lucas, daughter of an officer in the English army. She was an exceedingly lovely and brilliant girl, and made a great stir in the province. She was particularly admired by the wife of the Chief Justice, who said one day in jest :

" Rather than have Miss Lucas return home, I will myself step out of the way, and let her take my place."

Within a few months after uttering these words she died, and soon after her death the Chief Justice actually married .Miss Lucas. This lady was one of the greatest benefactors South Carolina ever had ; for, besides being an example of all the virtues and graces which adorn the female character, it was she who introduced into the province the cultivation of rice. In addition to the other services which she rendered her adopted home, she gave birth to the two brothers Pinckney, who are of most note in the general history of the country. The elder of these was Charles Cotesworth Pinckney, born in 1746, and the younger was Thomas, born in 1750.

When these two boys were old enough to begin their education, their father, the Chief Justice, like a good father as he was, went with them to England, accompanied by all his family, and there resided for many years, while they were at school ; for at that day there were no means of education in South Carolina. The boys were placed at Westminster school in London, and completed their studies at the University of Oxford. After leaving the University they began the study of the law in London, and were pursuing their studies there, or just beginning practice, when the troubles preceding the Revolutionary War hastened their return to their native land. They had been absent from their country twenty-one years, and were much gratified on reaching Charleston to witness its prosperity and unexpected growth. The elder of these brothers could remember when the first planter's wagon was driven into Charleston. This was about the year 1753. Pointing to this wagon one day, his father said to him :

"Charles, by the time you are a man, I don't doubt there will be at least twenty wagons coming to town."

Often in after life, when he would meet a long string of wagons in the country loaded with cotton or rice, he would relate this reminiscence of his childhood, and add :

" How happy my father would have been in the growth and prosperity of Carolina!"

These young men from the beginning of the Stamp Act agitation, when they were just coming of age, sympathized warmly with their oppressed countrymen on the other side of the ocean, and soon after their return home they entered the Continental army and served gallantly throughout the war. In 1780 we find Charles Cotesworth Pinckney writing to his wife in the following noble strain :

" Our friend, Philip Neyle was killed by a cannon-ball coming through one of the embrasures ; but I do not pity him, for he has died nobly in the defense of his country ; but I pity his aged father, now unhappily bereaved of his beloved and only child."

To one of his young friends he wrote soon after :

" If I had a vein that did not beat with love for my country, I myself would open it. If I had a drop of blood that could flow dishonorably, I myself would let it out."

It was the fortune of both these brothers to be held for a long time by the enemy as prisoners of war. The elder was captured upon the surrender of Charleston. The younger was desperately wounded at the battle of Camden, and was about to be transfixed by a bayonet, when a British officer who had known him at college recognized his features, and cried out in the nick of time :

" Save Tom Pinckney !"

The uplifted bayonet was withheld, and the wounded man was borne from the field a prisoner.

After the peace, General C. C. Pinckney was a member of the convention which framed our Constitution. During the Presidency of General Washington, he declined, first a seat upon the bench of the Supreme Court, and twice declined entering the cabinet. During the last year of Washington's administration, he accepted the appointment of

Minister to France, and it was while residing in Paris, that he uttered a few words which will probably render his name immortal. He was associated with Chief Justice Marshall and Elbridge Gerry, and their great object was to prevent a war between the United States and France. It was during the reign of the corrupt Directory that they performed this mission ; and Talleyrand, the Minister of War, gave them to understand that nothing could be accomplished in the way of negotiation unless they were prepared to present to the government a large sum of money. The honest Americans objecting to this proposal, Talleyrand intimated to them that they must either give the money or accept the alternative of war. Then it was that the honest and gallant Charles Cotesworth Pinckney uttered the words which Americans will never forget till they have ceased to be worthy of their ancestors :

" War be it, then !" exclaimed General Pinckney, " Millions for defense, sir ; but not a cent for tribute !"

On his return to the United States, war being imminent with France, he was appointed a Major-general in the army, and in the year 1800 he was a candidate for the Presidency. He lived to the year 1825, when he died at Charleston at the age of seventy-nine.

His brother Thomas was the Governor of South Carolina in 1789, and in 1792 was appointed by General Washington Minister to Great Britain. After residing some years in England, he was sent to Spain, where he negotiated the important treaty which secured us the free navigation of the Mississippi. After his return home, he served several years in Congress on the Federal side, and then retired to private life. During the war of 1812, he received the commission of Major-general, and served under General Jackson at the celebrated battle of Horseshoe Bend, where the power of the Creek Indians was broken forever.

He died at Charleston in 1828, aged seventy-eight years. Besides these Pinckneys there was a noted Charles Pinckney, a nephew of Chief Justice Pinckney, who was also captured when Charleston surrendered, remained a prisoner until near the close of the war, and afterwards bore a distinguished part in public life. He may be distinguished from others of his name from his being a democrat, an active adherent of Thomas Jefferson. He served as Minister to Spain during Mr. Jefferson's administration, and was four times elected Governor of South Carolina.

Finally, there was a Henry Laurens Pinckney, son of the Governor Pinckney last mentioned, born in 1794. For sixteen years he was a member of the Legislature of South Carolina, and was afterwards better known as editor and proprietor of the Charleston *Mercury*, a champion of State rights, and afterwards of nullification. During the nullification period, he was Mayor of Charleston, an office to which he was three times re-elected.

Thus the Pinckneys may be distinguished as follows: Thomas Pinckney, the founder; Charles Pinckney, the Chief Justice; Charles Cotesworth Pinckney, the Ambassador and candidate for the Presidency; Thomas Pinckney, General in the war of 1812; Charles Pinckney, the democrat; and Henry Laurens Pinckney, editor and author.